George Browning

The Edda Songs and Sagas of Iceland

Antigonos

George Browning

The Edda Songs and Sagas of Iceland

Unveränderter Nachdruck der Originalausgabe von 1876.

1. Auflage 2024 | ISBN: 978-3-38634-564-4

Antigonos Verlag ist ein Imprint der Outlook Verlagsgesellschaft mbH.

Verlag: Outlook Verlag GmbH, Zeilweg 44, 60439 Frankfurt, Deutschland, info@outlook-verlag.de
Vertretungsberechtigt: E. Roepke, Zeilweg 44, 60439 Frankfurt, Deutschland
Druck: Libri Plureos GmbH, Friedensallee 273, 22763 Hamburg, Deutschland

THE
EDDA SONGS AND SAGAS

OF

ICELAND.

A Lecture

DELIVERED AT

ST. GEORGE'S HALL, LANGHAM PLACE,

FEBRUARY, 1876.

BY

GEORGE BROWNING,

Member of the Icelandic Literary Society;

Author of 'Footprints,' 'Memoir of Napoleon III.,' &c. &c.

SECOND EDITION.

LONDON:

R. FREEMANTLE, 39 GREAT MARLBOROUGH-STREET.

1876.

Price Sixpence.

SYLLABUS.

Introductory remarks.

Intellectual condition of Iceland in the 11th, 12th, and 13th centuries. The Icelandic Republic.

Ari Fróði—Sæmundur Fróði—Snorri Sturluson.

What are the Eddas?

The Elder or Poetical Edda—The Younger or Prose Edda.

Northern Myths — Comparisons between Old Northern Poetry and that of Greece, Arabia, Persia, &c.

The Sagas—Derivation of the word "Saga."

Icelandic MSS.—The Royal Library of Copenhagen —The University Library of Copenhagen—Arne Magnæan Collection.

References to Great Britain, Ireland, and America contained in the Sagas—Old St. Paul's—St. Olave's Church, Southwark—Tooley Street, &c. (Harald Haardrada's Saga)—Northmen at the Court of Athelstan (Egils Saga)—Discovery of Greenland by the Icelanders (Eyrbyggja Saga), and of America in the 10th Century (Thorfinn's Saga)—Columbus in Iceland.

HISTORIC DATES.

A.D.

First Settlers in Iceland . . .	874
Landnáma Tið, or Period of the Colonisation	874-930
Stormy Feudal Times . . .	930-1030
Introduction of Christianity . .	1000
Skálds or Poets sung of the deeds in the previous turbulent period .	1030-1120
Golden period of Icelandic Literature .	1120-1260
Fall of the Icelandic Republic . .	1264
Iceland becomes a dependency of the Norwegian Crown.	
Iceland becomes a dependency of the Danish Crown .	1380
Cessation of an Original Literature, about . . . , . .	1400

EDDA SONGS AND SAGAS

OF

ICELAND.

ICELAND is a land of Song and of Saga as well as of frost and fire.

In that far-off Northern isle—that ultima Thule of modern civilisation—barren, bleak, and dreary, but yet possessing some grand phenomena of nature, grander than are to be seen in any other part of Europe, there sprang up a literature during the days of the Icelandic Republic—a literature rich, glowing, and glorious, unique in its way—a literature that hands down to posterity traditions from the earliest times.

And beyond these traditions that are to be found in the two Eddas there are in the Sagas complete pictures of what life was in the first centuries succeeding the colonisation of Iceland. Iceland, as you know, was colonised by the expatriated Norwegian Folk-kings Ingolfur and Leif, who had been dispossessed of their lands by the superior force of Harald Haarfager, or Harold Fair Hair, who for the love of Gyda, the daughter of the King of Hardaland, vowed never to clip his beard nor comb his hair until he had brought the whole of Norway under one head, as Eric had done in Sweden, Gorm in Denmark, and Egbert in Saxon England. This unification of Norway took place in 872 and the colonisation of Iceland in 874.

With their language these Norwegian settlers brought over the sea to their new island home their mythology, their national ideas, their superstitions, and their folk-lore.

At all times story-telling has been a favourite occupation of the Icelanders, and is so still in the present day. To tell a story well was considered a great accomplishment, and to deviate from the truth next door to a crime. Even the Icelanders of the present day tell with a simplicity of language and clearness of style all about the great deeds that have happened in their native land, in their " Gamla Isafold," six, seven, or eight centuries ago, what great men were their forefathers; but they know little about the geography or history of modern Europe. To travel in Iceland at the present day, and have the interesting points here and there—at Mosfell, at Thingvellir, at Haukedal, and at Skál-holt—shown to us by the peasants, who have their own history as recorded in the Sagas at their fingers' ends, creates for the traveller at once an intense interest in Northern Saga-lore.

During the long winter evenings it is still the custom for the family to gather round in a circle, while the father reads these historical narratives aloud to the women who are spinning and the children who are combing the wool; the male part of the population occupy themselves at these family gatherings either in mending their nets or helping the women to spin.

While children are yet young, they hear these Sagas read over and over again, and so as they grow older they take in them a deeper interest, until they get quite to love them, and to know them by heart for life.

In the summer-time, when they ride out on short excursions from one farm to another, the distance between the farms being frequently thirty to forty miles, they talk with their companions about the

great and glorious deeds of their renowned ancestors;
they go far out of their way to see again, though they
have seen it twenty times before, the spot where
some great feast had been held or some wrong
avenged, and they embrace and weep over the glory
and valour and majesty of their forefathers as re-
counted in their best-beloved books—the Sagas.

These writings, to an Icelandic farmer's mind, are
like "harðr fiskur" and "skyr" to his body—the
length and breadth of sustenance. Without these
Sagas the Icelandic "bœr," or farm-house, would
indeed be dull.

This sentimental pathos about the deeds of their
ancestors is rather absurd, nearly as absurd as if the
English were to weep when they met about the loss
of Harold the Saxon, at Hastings, the woes and trials
of his glorious predecessor King Alfred, or, to come
to later times, the terrible loss England sustained by
the smothering of the two babes in the Tower.

Iceland, we have said, is a land of song—song not
in the modern sense of the term, some little musical
recreation to pass away pleasantly ten minutes, but
in a grand and serious sense were these Edda songs
of the Icelanders looked upon by the whole population of the North during the active and warlike and
tempestuous times, when the Scandinavian Vikings
played the most important rôle in European history.

At this early period, from the 8th to the 10th
century, the art of writing in Latin character had not
yet been introduced into Northern Europe. It was
only after these turbulent sea-roving spirits had
settled down in their respective homes, and a gene-
ration or two had passed away, that these cycles of
songs came to find their way on to the dried skins of
the sheep, written with an ink that the Icelanders
prepared from a plant (icel. *lyng*) growing on their
wild, bleak, and barren lava-strewn plains. The
earliest specimen of Icelandic penmanship extant is
from about the year 1150 A.D. Before that time,

then the Scandinavians kept their records in runes, cut into the rocks, and upon tablets of wood.

The latter, from these early times, have been long since destroyed; but concerning runes, despite the admonition of the wise woman in Völuspà, "*skalat maðr rúnir rista,*" (with runes no man should meddle), a most exhaustive work has recently appeared, compiled by the able and distinguished scholar George Stephens, Professor of Early and Modern English at the University of Copenhagen.

Now with regard to the early intellectual condition in Iceland during the period of the Icelandic Republic.

At a time when there was a dark cloud of superstition and ignorance hanging over the European horizon, a century or two before the days when Dante and Petrarca re-awakened Europe with their immortal song, and Boccaccio remodelled the beautiful Italian language by his elegant prose, the Icelanders were basking in the full sunlight of literature and revelling in the glories of a free constitution.

Here, in our own country, the trial by jury and a free Parliament are the two important features that we have borrowed from the culture and civilisation of early Icelandic times.

From the 11th to the 13th century is the most flourishing period of Icelandic literature, the period that commences with Ari Fróði, the first Icelandic historian, and ends with Snorri Sturluson and his nephews Sturli Thórðarson and Olaf Hvítaskáld.

The Icelandic Republic came to be broken up by violent family feuds that involved the murder of Snorri at Reykholt, and the handing over of the reins of government to the Norwegian king, Hákon Hákonsson, in the year 1264 A.D.

With the fall of the Republic, the pride and glory of the Icelanders faded away, and her *littérateurs* sunk down into mere collators of previously written MSS. Their warriors became dreams of the past, their skálds or poets disappeared, and we hear no more of that wonderful activity that thrust them so prominently before the eyes of mediæval Europe. Nor is this in any way to be wondered at; the Icelanders simply shared the same fate common to other nations that have left a distinctive mark on the history of the civilisation of the world.

The age of the Vikings and the age of the priests did not harmonise in the slightest degree.

After the introduction of Christianity, in the year 1000 A.D., by formal declaration in an assembly of the Althing, Paganism still lingered for several centuries in the hearts of the people. Certainly they were required to eat their horse-flesh in private, and forbidden by law to expose the newly-born children. Those were two old Pagan customs; the former appears to have little meaning in a religious point of view, seeing that in a Christian land it was on the eve of revival in the 19th century: the latter was done to ensure a race of fine healthy children, sound in limb and lung, for in those days the entire male population were warriors, and weak sickly warriors were what a Northern Pagan particularly despised. No wonder, then, old Pagan times generated a grand, tall, robust race of men, seeing that the parents were willing to sacrifice so much life for the sake of breed. In Niála, one of the oldest and most interesting of Icelandic Sagas, these Pagan customs are fully explained.

In modern times they would appear cruel, perhaps, but their cruelty in a great degree vanishes when the strong, healthy, warlike tone of the age is taken into consideration, and what an object, therefore, it became to look after only the "survival of the fittest." The chief characteristic of the Northern spirit was belief in his own might (trúa á mátt sinn ok megin). A Northern warrior—and, as before said, in the Pagan times all were more or less warriors—never left unchallenged an insult or a wrong, and fought

up to the last gasp. The story of the two lovers of
the chaste and beautiful Helga will serve as a good
illustration of this, and will be found in Gunnlaug's
Saga Ormstúnga, or the Saga of Gunnlaug Snake-
tongue. This is one of the earliest and best written,
as well as the most romantic in Northern Saga-lore.

The Vikings of the North belonged only to a time,
and to a time that does not come again; they were
entirely a race apart these Vikings, and they per-
formed a history, and the skálds of those times wrote
down that history in the old Northern tongue. Englishmen are the true heirs of the spirit of the Vikings,
and in a practical way they have made use of that
heir-loom, especially in the days of good Queen Bess,
when English ships were fearlessly cruising in every
sea, and English sailor-kings were the first to sail
round the world. Byron was essentially a type of
the old Northern Vikings, although born seven or
eight centuries after they had ceased to exist. And
this old Viking spirit is not yet dead among us; as
an instance of this we have only to point to the bold
and adventurous expedition that has so recently left
our shores on a voyage of discovery to the Polar
Seas.

The Icelandic Republic was an outgrowth of the
military hierarchy adopted in Iceland soon after its
colonisation, under the political leadership of a Goði,
or warrior-priest.

It was found necessary, however, to establish a
settled code of laws, and Ulfljót, one of these Goðar,
although in his sixtieth year, undertook a voyage to
Norway, in order to gain a thorough knowledge of
the science and practice of jurisprudence. He studied
carefully the "Gulathing" code, at that time in
force in Norway. On his return in 927, he immediately made a tour round the island, and put before
the inhabitants the advisability of framing and adopt-
ing a law code applicable to their local and peculiar
requirements, and at a general meeting convened at

Thingvellir, in the south-western part of the island, in
the following year, this spot was chosen as the annual
meeting place of the National Assembly, and this
code of laws was, by the unanimous consent of the
nation, declared to be the law of the land. At this
same meeting the Icelanders formed themselves into
a regularly constituted Republic that flourished for
nearly four hundred years, and under which the
glorious Icelandic literature grew up.

The general assembly of the nation was called the
Althing, and met annually for the space of sixteen
days on the plains of Thingvellir. The president of
the assembly bore the title of Lögsögumaðr, or
speaker of the law (literally, law-say-man).

One of the most remarkable features in the deve-
lopment of Icelandic literature—one that influenced
it in an extraordinary degree—was the formation of
schools or seats of learning, serving in their time the
same educational ends as the Universities that subsequently sprang up in all parts of Europe.

Of these schools there were four in Iceland. The
first was founded by Bishop Isleif, in the early part
of the 11th century, at Skálholt, and this became the
mother of the other three schools, viz., at Haukedal,
at Oddi, and at Hólum. The school at Haukedal,
conducted by Hallr, who was born in 996, and bap-
tized when three years old, by Thángbrand, the
first preacher of Christianity in Iceland, was the
most celebrated and the most ancient after the before-
mentioned school at Skálholt. The school at Oddi
was set up by Sæmundur Fróði, and that at Hólum
by Jón Ogmundsson, his friend. The education at
these groves of Academia was of a peculiar kind,
but one entirely in harmony with the age. Let us
take the last-mentioned school at Hólum as an
illustration of the kind of education current in Iceland in the 11th and 12th centuries. All were taught
to read and write: that was essential in those days,
in fact little girls were told that unless they learnt at

a very early age to read and write they would never
get married. Now let us look how wide was the
range of accomplishments in those early Icelandic
times. At Hólum there were but two masters—the
one gave instruction in Latin, the other in poetry
and music. A very simple but a very beautiful kind
of education, rather different from the schooling
fashionable at the present day, when steam, the
monarch of the age, has multiplied so vastly the
means of communication that nations, formerly unknown to one another, are now next-door neighbours
as it were, thus forcing upon the children of to-day
more learning than their brains can digest, so that
there must necessarily be a superficiality in the ac-
quirements that would have startled and shocked the
early Icelanders, even as we are startled by the at
first sight apparent incompleteness of an early
Northern education.

But, on the other hand, what a wide field does not
history embrace, and the Scalds of the North were,
as we shall see by-and-bye, the historians of the age.
The world is made up of contraries, and it is a curious
fact that so soon as a nation advances in civilisation so
far as to write down the spoken language, the language
itself begins to deteriorate, loses gradually its strength,
vigour, and power, and becomes every day a more
practical language rather than one of beauty, harmony, and strength.

ARI FRÓÐI.—Ari Thorgilsson, called more commonly Ari Fróði, or the Learnèd, was the first
to write in the Icelandic vernacular (á norrænu
máli).

Born in 1067, he studied in Hallr's school at
Haukedal, from his seventh to his twenty-first year.
Ari Fróði is the author of one of the most important
books in connection with the early history of Iceland.
It is called the Islendingabók (Schedæ islandiæ
libellus), and was completed about the year 1134
A.D. It contains a short historical account of Iceland

from its colonisation to the beginning of the twelfth century.

The laws of Iceland, up to the year 1117 A.D., had been kept in the memory of the lögsögumaðr or law-sayman, but in that year it was agreed by common consent of the Althing that the time had now come when they should no longer be trusted to memory. Ari was consulted in the matter, and in conjunction with the rune-learned Thórodd was deputed to write down in the vernacular the legal code that had been in force since the days of Ulfljót, and the foundation of the Icelandic Republic.

SÆMUNDUR FRÓÐI.—Sæmundur Sigfússon, whose name has been connected with the Elder Edda, but erroneously, was a contemporary of Ari Fróði, and one of the most learned Icelanders of his day. At an early age Sæmundur left Iceland and wandered for many years far and wide over Europe, particularly in Germany and France. He studied at the then most flourishing University of Erfurt and subsequently found his way to Paris, where he was accidentally met by his countryman, Jón Ogmundsson*, who persuaded him to return to his native land.

They set out together from Paris—the high seat of learning at that time in Europe—and reached Iceland in 1076.

When all the monastic world was covering parchments with the language of the priests—Latin—it is a curious fact that the Icelanders employed the vernacular, and it is this peculiarity that gives to Icelandic literature a double importance.

More than one learnèd authority has been pleased to call the Anglo-Saxons the schoolmasters of the Icelanders, in that the poems of Beowulf and Cædmon had encouraged them to make use of the vernacular in writing down their records —their Songs, Sagas, and Laws, that throw so much

---

* Jón Ogmundsson became First Bishop of Hólum A.D. 1105.

light upon the traditions and history of Europe in the Middle Ages.

There is this difference, however, between the Anglo-Saxon and the Icelandic literature — the former with few exceptions has been destroyed— eaten by time, burned by fanatics, or trodden under foot by ransackers of convents—while the latter, owing principally to the solitary position of Iceland and the hitherto little opened-up communication between Iceland and the rest of Europe—has been wonderfully preserved.

But beyond this there were opportunities for the creating of a great national literature entirely exceptional.

Anglo-Saxon Literature, owing to the early introduction of Christianity into England, was nipped, as it were, in the bud; but in Iceland it was several centuries later—not until the year 1000 A.D.—that Paganism nominally made way for Christianity, and in reality lingered in the religious and social customs of the people for several subsequent centuries.

In the Sagas it is mentioned that Sæmundur during his travels in Germany had been initiated into the mysteries of the *svarta skóla*, or black school—for all this necromancing, alchemy, and what was then called "Egyptian sorceries," were much in vogue in Europe at that time—and those who had practised in that school were looked upon with a certain amount of awe; in fact, Sæmundur, after his return, was regarded by many of his countrymen as a kind of Dr. Faustus in league with the devil.

SNORRI STURLUSON—One of the most remarkable men that Iceland, or even Europe, has ever known was Snorri Sturluson, the warrior, the statesman, and the poet, born in Iceland in 1178. When three years old he was placed under the care of Jón Loptsson, then carrying on the school founded by Sæmundur at Oddi. There he remained until his nineteenth year. Snorri married a rich wife, Herdís, daughter of a priest called Bersi the Rich. Her marriage-portion was 4,000 rigsdalers in silver, a considerable sum in those days. Snorri's worldly wealth at that time consisted of 160 rigsdalers. After his marriage he rapidly rose to a prominent position, socially and politically, and was four times elected President of the Althing. Few, if any, of his countrymen could equal him in wealth and splendour, and often to the Althing he rode accompanied by a retinue of eight or nine hundred armed men.

These Northern warriors were richly clad—their forefathers, some of them, had served in the Varangian guard of the Byzantine Emperors, and so had become acquainted with the splendour and magnificence of an Imperial Eastern Court. But the great pride of the Northman lay in his bright breast-plate, burnished helm, and glittering spear.

Many times he visited Norway, and allowed himself to be fêted by the King Hákon Hákonsson, who was trying to bring Iceland under Norwegian rule. Snorri aided Hákon in his schemes simply to satisfy his own ambition, for by turning traitor to his country he anticipated being made a Norwegian Jarl. In this, however, he was disappointed, and left Norway in disgust, against the expressed wish of Hákon, the king. Skúli Jarl had stirred up a small kind of rebellion against the throne, and Snorri sided with Skúli Jarl. Hákon put down the rebellion, and in order to be revenged on Snorri, instigated some chieftain Icelanders to rise against the overpowering ambition and lust after wealth that Snorri had manifested, and among these was Gissur Thorwaldsson, who, with a small party of followers, fell upon Snorri at his estate at Reykholt, and murdered him there in cold blood on the 22nd September, 1241.

These are the chief points in Snorri's agitated and eventful political life.

His compilation of the Norwegian King's Saga, the so-called HEIMSKRÍNGLA, has a grand reputation in the Saga-literature of Iceland. The narrative is simple and his style elevated and free. There is a peculiar charm in Snorri's writings. As a historian he stands in the front rank. With contemporaneous writers, for instance, the monks Gunnlaug, and Odd who wrote Olaf Tryggvason's Saga, history is tinged with their admiration for the newly-introduced Christian religion, while in Snorri's writings we are hardly aware of the *person* of the author whether he be Pagan or Christian, friend or foe.

Heimskríngla is a simply told narrative of historical events that happened in Norway, and the purity of style, simplicity of language, and truth to fact none of his successors ever attained. His works are therefore valuable as models. In conjunction with his nephew Olaf Hvítaskáld, Snorri Sturluson compiled the Younger or Prose Edda, sometimes called Snorri's Edda, as in its compilation he had the lion's share.

Now with regard to the Eddas. The meaning of the word Edda has been differently interpreted. The most generally accepted idea until more recent times was that the word signified Mother or Mother of mothers (Oldemoder, or Allmother), but now in the Scandinavian lands, where the study of the old Northern classical language and literature has in latter times made wonderful progress, the term Edda is attributed to an old Teutonic word signifying art, (*Art and Weise*, for example; in the way and manner of). This is the general opinion at Copenhagen, and also that held by the distinguished German philologist, Jacob Grimm.

In the ancient Songs and Sagas of Iceland the foretelling woman (icel. *spákona*) plays a conspicuous part, and some suppose that the word Edda may have originally meant a wise woman, analogous to the Greek sybil. It has been sought to trace out, then, the origin of the Eddaic songs to the recitations of enthusiastic or inspired prophetesses or spákonur; but this idea has not many supporters.

The Elder Edda is the most interesting relic that the Icelanders have handed down to us. It contains the cosmogony and theogony, as viewed from a Northern standpoint, and in many of the songs may be discerned the far remote connection between Scandinavia and the East, many of the Aryan myths being distinctly traceable in this early record of old Northern times. The songs of the Elder Edda may be divided into two categories—the mythic and the heroic—the former treating of the origin and fate of the universe, and the latter the dawn of social life throughout the Teutonic world.

The heroic songs run parallel with the old German traditions described in the famous Niebelungen, the oldest semi-historical Teutonic record extant.

For a long time it was thought that Sæmundur Fróði was the author of these Edda songs. This, however, is disproved by referring to Olaf Tryggvason's Saga, where it may be seen that four of these lyric epics were sung at the Norwegian Court sixty years before the birth of Sæmundur Sigfússon (1056 A.D.) Atlamál is also known to have existed before his time.

Then it was stated that Sæmundur, during his travels in Germany, had found these ancient cycles of song referring to the traditions of the Volsungs, the Gjukungs, and the Niflungs; and that he himself put them into Northern verse on his return to Iceland.

From the contents of these Edda songs we can assert most confidently that they have come to be composed at different periods and by different skálds. According to more recent criticism, however, Sæmundur is not in any way connected with the Elder Edda, and his name appears simply to have been attached to the Codex Regius by Bishop Sveinsson, who first discovered this most important MS. in one of the farm-houses on the ecclesiastical property at Skálholt, and, for the sake of giving the book a grand name, before sending it as a gift to the Danish King Frederic III. at Copenhagen, called it Edda Sæmundar hinns Fróða.

These Edda songs contain wonderful illustrations of the passion intensity in the Northern breast differing from the passion intensity of the Greeks in that their's was an outburst overwhelming its victims with the force of the avalanche, while the Northern spirit brooded over in silence—even with a smile on the lips—wrongs inflicted, and, thus masked, thought out the most sure, the most bitter, the most satisfying revenge.

Women play a great *rôle* in the Northern tragic life. Lady Macbeths were not at all uncommon in the stirring period of Icelandic history.

With a Pagan indifference to life, the Northern warrior was unmindful of after-happenings or results; where an injury had been inflicted, their duty it was to revenge, regardless of how such revenge would react subsequently on themselves.

The Northern spirit is not attractive at first glance like that of Hellas, but the more its intricacies are studied the more the beauties stand forth and entrance.

The energetic harmony of these old poems has a great charm; the most ancient are the simplest and most beautiful. The original verses have no final rhymes, but trust to alliteration and assonance for their strength.

In the grand ethic poem, Hávamál, or Song of the Highest, we are supposed to be listening to the words of Odin, and hear how the great God grapples with Fate. This gnome poem contains the sum and substance of the old Northern world-wisdom and life-rules. Then come the Heroic, that might well be called Mythic-Heroic songs, and they treat particularly of the times of the great migrations.

The *dramatis personæ* frequently make mention of Southern men and women, of the sun mountains, and so on, but that these old Teutonic traditions came to be generally current in Scandinavia there can be no doubt, and after getting in some degree acclimatised, were written down centuries after the events therein described had actually taken place. Through all the songs there is a wild and weird passion-current running that brings about the destruction of all who take part in these violent ebullitions of love and hatred, jealousy and revenge.

The Edda Songs have little in common with the Homeric poems — a resemblance that has often, without reason, been found. There is, however, a comparison with the Greek literature that may be made, and it is with the Greek drama, especially with Greek tragedy. There is this difference between the Heroic Poems of the North and those of Greece: while the latter are purely epic, the former abound with a strong lyrical element, and the lyric beauty of these epic poems entitles them to the name of lyric-epic. In classic form and word-paintings these heroic songs—Sigurd Fâfnisbane's, Guðrun's song, Brynhilda's—stand above everything that has been handed down to us in the realm of Northern poetry. They are the classical trilogies of the North. Matter is not sacrificed to diction, nor diction to matter; they are fairly balanced, and there is a healthy harmony of dramatic construction pervading the whole. A dark destiny hovers over the ring of action, and exacts not only the life of individuals, but of entire families or tribes. Passion, in all its terrible forms and fearful extravagances, reaches at one time the horrible, at another the sublime.

In those days, as now—the world in reality has changed very little—treasures brought about strife. It was the treasures of Sigurd Fâfnisbane that brought about the deadly strife between the Volsungs and Niflungs. Sigurd loses his heart to the daughter of Budli, King of the Huns—the amazon Brynhilda,

who was a sister of Atli (Attila)—but his bridal vows
are broken by the sorceries of the intriguing Queen
Grimhilda, who has determined that Sigurd should
marry her daughter Gudrun. There is a beautiful
passage in the great song of Gudrun that I will
quote.

For the death of Sigurd Gudrun is inconsolable,
and, what was still worse, could shed no tears. The
women round about her tried to console her as they
stood by Sigurd's bier, and they, in turn, commenced
to tell what sorrows they had outlived.

> Gold-clad, goodly brides
> Of the greatest earls
> Sat by Gudrun.
> Each told her
> The sorest grief
> They had outlived.
> Then said Gjáflung,
> Gjúki's daughter,
> Myself I trow
> To be the most wretched.
> Five husbands
> Have I lost,
> Two daughters
> And three sisters,
> Eight brothers;
> I am left alone.

Still Gudrun's grief was so deep, her heart was so
sorrow-swollen and well-nigh to bursting, for she
could shed no tears.

> Then said Herborg,
> Hunland's Queen,
> "I a greater
> Grief may boast.
> My seven sons
> In southern parts,
> And husband—the eighth—
> In battle perished.
> My parents both,
> And brethren four,
> Wind and wave
> Carried away;
> And a cruel sea
> Sank the ship.

I searched them myself,
Myself I found them,
And in the earth myself
I laid their remains.
This I went through
In one single year,
And no one to comfort me.

Next thro' warfare
Was I kept as thrall.
Every morning
Was I bid to dress,
And to tie the sandals
Of, my master's wife.

With jealous words
She wrung my heart,
And dealt me blows
In bitter wrath.
Never did I know
A better master,
Nor a worse mistress."

Still Gudrun's grief could find no vent; her heart was so choked, so sorrow-swollen, tears she could not shed.

Then said Goldrand,
Gjúki's daughter,
"Foster mother,
However skilful,
Still thou know'st not
How to soften
Sorrow's pangs
In a youthful heart."

And here Goldrand swept off the pall from Sigurd's corpse and threw it at the knees of Gudrun. Gudrun gazed at him, saw the noble head soiled with gore and the kingly skull cloven in two, and at once the locks were loosened, her cheeks coloured, and a rain of tears poured down her face, and she spoke. The danger of her heart bursting with grief was over. This intensity of grief, as well as the passion intensity that follows, find a reflection in King Lear and Macbeth.

And the birds all
In her bower
Took to joyous singing.

Then, quoth Gudrun,
Gjúki's daughter,
My Sigurd differed
From the sons of Gjúki
As a towering tree
From tender herbs.
I, too, was valued
Above other women.
Now he is departed,
I am nothing more
Than a leaf in autumn.

Then Brynhilda, who during Sigurd's lifetime was burning with jealousy for Gudrun, now he was dead, wished her no good, as may be seen by the few following lines.

Quoth Brynhilda,
Budli's daughter,
May that woman lack
Mate and issue
Who taught thee Gudrun
Tears to shed.
And this morning
Thy tongue hath untied.

But these Edda songs should be read in the original before they can be thoroughly appreciated; still in these translations the workings of the passions of the human breast—love, grief, hatred, &c., that in the Northern spirit assumes a terrible intensity—are here well exemplified.

The Eddas also are full of metaphorical expressions; for instance, a good and virtuous man is referred to as " a tree of gold," with an eye, as it were, to the old Northern tradition that men were fashioned out of wood, not with the idea at all that real trees had any connection whatever with gold; a brave warrior is spoken of in Helgakviða as an " oak of battle." Nowadays, when we associate a man with wood, we call him a " stick," not quite so flattering

an appellation as an oak of battle; but then that may
be the fault of the age.

Now let us take some of the myths in the Younger
Edda in order to show how remarkable and attractive
are these poetic remnants of antiquity.

The creation of mankind occurred in this manner, according to the Northern mythology. The sons of Bórs
—Odin, Vele, and Ve—found on the beach two trees,
whereof they created men. Odin gave soul and life;
Vele understanding and movement; Ve countenance,
speech, hearing, and sight. They gave them clothes
and names; the man was called Ask and the woman
Embla.*

From Ask and Embla descends mankind. They
obtained Midgard as a dwelling-place. Night was a
daughter of the giant Narfi, dark as her progenitor;
she was married to Delling, of the race of the Asi,
or gods, and by him she had a son, Day, who was
light and beautiful as his father. Allfather, the
highest of the gods who dwelt in Gimli, gave Night
and Day two horses and two chariots, and set them
in heaven, in order that they might drive round over
the earth.

Night drives in front with the horse Rimfaxi (Rime-
mane); every morning drops drip from its bridle,
and this is the dew on the mountains and in the valleys.
Day is drawn by Skinfaxi (Light-mane); out of its
mane comes such a refulgence that it is sufficient to
give light to the whole earth and air. A man, by
the name of Mundilfori, begat a son and a daughter,
who were so beautiful that he called the son Moon,
and the daughter Sun. This aroused the jealousy
and the anger of the gods, who seized both son and
daughter and set them up in the heavens.

Sun is now being pursued by a giant in wolf's
clothing, so is always hastening on her course; and

---

* It is worthy of notice that the first letter of the first man should be
A, and that of the first woman should be E, in that respect correspond-
ing with our Adam and Eve.

another giant, also in wolf's clothing, runs after Moon.[*]

In the centre of the world the Asi built a castle, and called it Asgard. There dwelt the gods—the great Asi race. From heaven to earth they built a tri-coloured bridge, and gave to it the name of Bifröst. This is the rainbow.

Then we come to the golden age of Heathen mythology—the commencement of the fighting times.

The Asi met on the plain of Ida, within the castle-walls of Asgard, and began to build dwellings for the gods and goddesses. Gladsheim, the beautiful golden-beaming, was destined for the home of the gods; and the pretty dwelling, Vingólf, for the goddesses. They played games, were happy, and had abundance of gold. And the joy, the delights of this golden age, lasted until three mighty giants came from Jötunheim. Then the first homicide in the world took place. Odin cast his spear in among men, and this was the beginning of the fighting times.

Once upon a time, long, long ago, there reigned a wise king, by the name of Gylfi, who held the Asi in such reverence that he travelled over to Asgard to make their better acquaintance. As he entered the castle he perceived a hall; it was so lofty he could scarcely see its extent, and the ceiling was covered with golden shields. This was Valhalla.

Gylfi saw there many men, of whom some were playing, others drinking, and others again wrestling. He approached the high-seats whereon the lords of the castle were seated. They bade him welcome, and he soon told them for why he had undertaken the journey to Asgard. This is about the way the Younger Edda begins. Let us then imagine ourselves

---

[*] In Northern mythology the sun is always spoken of in the feminine gender and the moon in the masculine.

in the position of the Swedish King Gylfi, wishing to know something further about the old Northern mythology.

We shall make the acquaintance of a curious company—the Asi, the Asynies, the Nornes, Valkyrs, and Elves; Dwarfs, Trolls and Giants; but we will only stop to consider from among this crowd those the most important.

Odin is the Allfather, the eldest and the highest of the gods. Those who fall fighting are his beloved sons, and War is called Odin's play and the sword Odin's fire. He is the wisest of all the gods—in stature mighty, long-bearded, and one-eyed. His other eye he pawned for a drink from Mimer's well, the Well of Wisdom, with little chance of ever getting it back again. He owns a great hall in heaven called Valaskjálf, bedecked with bright silver, and his high seat is Hlídskjálf. From this seat he sees over the whole world. His horse—an eight-footed horse—Sleipnir carries him through the air and over the sea; he wears a blue mantle, a gold helmet, and carries a spear called Gúngnir. He takes no food, but wine: that is to him both meat and drink. Poetry is called Odin's mead. Hugin and Munin, his two ravens, are most useful birds; at break of day they bend their flight across the world to see what is going on, and bring the news to their master at his first morning meal. Out of golden vessels every day he drinks joyously with Saga in her dwelling; her dwelling is called Sökk-vabæk, and thereover the cool waves whisper.

Thor is Odin's son, the strongest of all the gods, and the defence of Asgard. There are 540 halls in Bilskirnir, his castle, the grandest in the world, and 800 warriors can march in abreast. His chariot is drawn by two he-goats; from the chariot-wheels proceed thunder and lightning.

Three precious treasures he owns—the hammer Mjölnir, the belt, and a pair of iron gloves. Thor's hammer has this wonderful property, that of finding its way back again into the caster's hand. It was frequently used by Thor to crush the heads of the Rimegiants.

Baldur is the god of Innocence, and is another of Odin's sons. His dwelling is called Breiðablik; there no unclean thing may enter. Nanna is the name of his wife.

Njord is the ruler of the sea, the governor of the winds and the flames, and is invoked by sailors and fishermen. He is rich and bestows riches. His dwelling, Nóatún, is on the sea.

Freyr is the son of Njord, beautiful and mighty, and the ruler of the sunshine and the rain. He scatters peace and prosperity about the earth, whose produce he has under his thumb. He reigns over Alfheim, the home of the spirit-elves.

Tyr, another of Odin's sons, is the god of battle, and rules the victory; for this reason it was considered lucky to march out to war on Tuesday (Tyrsdag).

Another son of Odin is Bragi, the god of poetry, renowned for his eloquence and his wisdom. His health frequently was drunk at feasts, and he was called the long-bearded Asa.

Heimdal is a great and good Asa. He is born by nine mothers, sisters. His teeth are of gold. He sees both by night and by day hundreds and hundreds of miles, needs less sleep than a bird, and hears the grass grow on the earth and the wool on the sheep's back. He is the guardian of the gods, and is called the White Asa. Bifröst, the mighty bridge stretching from earth to heaven, he guards against the mountain-giants, and has a horn that can be heard over the whole world. It is called Gjallarhorn.

Vali is another of Odin's sons; no one bolder than he in fight, and what is rather fortunate, he hits where he aims.

Ullir, a stepson of Thor, is a beautiful and a mighty giant, and an excellent skater.

Forseti is a son of Baldur; his hall is in heaven, it rests on pillars of gold and is bedecked with pure silver; he arranges all disputes.

The Asynies are the wives of the gods. Frig is the highest Asynie; Queen of the Asi and the Asynies, and Odin's wife. She owns the magnificent dwelling Fensalir. Fylla is her waiting woman, wears long flowing hair and a golden band about the head, she bears her mistress's toilet-box, looks after her boots, and hears her secrets. Gná is her messenger, having at her command a horse capable of darting through the air, and flying over the sea.

Freya is involved in love affairs, and love-songs please her; she is the daughter of the Vane Njord, and so is called Vanadis. She was once married to Od, by whom she had a daughter the beautiful Hnos. Od, however, left his spouse and Freya wept golden tears, so that the poets called her the tear-beautiful goddess. She disguised herself, under many different names, and wandered far and wide among unknown nations in search of Od but could not find him. She owns the castle Folkvang, the neck ornament Brising, and a pair of magic wings. She drives in a chariot drawn by a couple of cats.

From her name comes the glorious name of Frúe, Germ. *Frau*, English *mistress*, in the old-fashioned sense of the word—matron—married woman. Lofn is amiable and good, and influences Odin to remove obstacles that stand in the way of lovers coming together.

Var respects men and women's love-vows and takes revenge on those who are faithless. Broken vows cannot be hidden from her and revenge comes swiftly.

Gefion is a virgin, and those who die as virgins serve her.

Sif, the beautiful-hair'd goddess, is Thor's wife.

Idun is the wife of Bragi, but of elfish extraction.

She keeps in a casket the apples whereof the gods eat, when they grow old, in order to become young again.

Eir is the best physician.

Syn guards the doors of the hall and locks those out who may not enter.

The Nornes and the Valkyrs are very important personages in Northern Mythology.

Under the ash of Yggdrasil, at the well of Urd, stands a beautiful castle, wherefrom there came forth three wise virgins, Urd, Verdandi, and Skuld. These virgins decide men's lifetime and fate, and are therefore called Nornes. Urd is the Norne of thé Past, Verdandi of the Present, and Skuld of the Future. Besides these there are others who come to each new-born child. There are both good and evil Nornes. The Valkyrs are called the Maids of Odin, and are sent by him to every battle. They choose out those who shall fall, and rule the victory; they are young and beautiful, and helm-bedecked, with blood-stained breastplates, glittering spears and shining shields; they ride amid lightning through the air, and over the sea.

This, then, is but a rapid sketch or glance at the *dramatis personæ* of Northern Mythology that any of you are likely to meet with, if you set out as we did, with King Gylfi, on a journey to Asgard.

It is, however, but the prologue; for the play, where the adventures, combats, heart-burnings of the gods and goddesses keep Asgard in constant commotion, we would refer you to the Eddas themselves.

Goethe was well acquainted with the stories to be found in the Eddas, and in his *Wahrheit und Dichtung* says :—" From these fictions such a pleasant impression has remained with me, that they belong to the most valuable things which my imagination can recall."

The nature-worship of the North finds its counterpart in the Persian Zendavesta. That the Persian language is nearly related, as well with the Northern as with the Indian, is well known, and even as Northern Mythology is indebted to Oriental ideas and traditions, so is old Northern art. Carpets and saddle-cloths, worked by hand to-day up country in Iceland, wear the Arabian pattern, and the silver ornaments and dresses still worn by the Icelandic peasants on high days and holidays bear a remarkable resemblance to certain silver ornaments and national costumes from India, Persia, and Egypt.

THE SAGAS* are historical narratives, and form a valuable and, for the most part, authentic record of the social and political life in mediæval Northern Europe. The learned Torfæus puts down their number at 187 ; P. E. Müller, author of the well-known work the ' Sagabibliothek,' at 156, but to fix the number of these records is quite immaterial.

They are a recital of heroic deeds and active warfaring and domestic life, and there runs through them a strongly-developed sense of freedom and love of independence so dear to the Northern mind.

Let us see what were the social and political aims of a Northern warrior. First and foremost the Northern spirit abhorred despotism, loved a free, vigorous, independent life, and beyond being king of his own ship, chief in his own district, and master in his own house, his ambition did not soar. But with less a true Northern warrior-spirit was seldom content.

And why are these Sagas so grand, so important, so unique ?

Running through the whole there is a peculiar talent found in no other literature—a strong, healthy, warlike tone; and, speaking more particularly of the earlier written Sagas, they afford an opportunity for the study of the human character not to be found in a like degree in any other literature. Winding in and out of the social, political, and domestic life so

---

* The word Saga comes from segja, to say, to tell, to narrate.

graphically described in these early Icelandic writings are the human passions in all their varied forms, thus offering an insight, as it were, into the breasts of strong and weak, rich and poor, grave and gay. For the most part, the Sagas are original records of passing events during the Middle Ages—events occurring not only in Iceland, but also in other parts of Europe —in Norway, Sweden, Denmark, Great Britain, the Orkneys, Shetland, and Ireland. There are also references to the part taken by the Northmen in the Crusade Wars, and how many of these northern Jarls, and even kings, served in the Varangian guard of the Byzantine Emperors, and came back from Constantinople — called Mikligard in the Sagas—laden with spoil to their Northern homes. In Harald Haardrada's Saga may be found grand descriptions of these Viking expeditions in the Mediterranean, as he himself, Harald Haardrada, King of Norway, was at one time captain of the Latin Emperor's body-guard. Those were the days when the horses were shod with shoes of gold, and the trappings of a magnificence that in modern times can only be found in the East.

With regard to outward show, the Northern warrior cared little for this beyond the trustiness and beauty of his weapons and the richness of his dress. His dwelling and drinking halls were patterns of simplicity, the walls and roof of the latter were covered with shields, but there was entirely lacking the effeminating influences of an Eastern Court.

The Sagas, up to the so-called Sturlunga period (Sturlúnga tíð), were a record, not of fictions, but of events. After the fall of the glorious Icelandic Republic, when Iceland, through intrigue both at home and abroad, became an apanage of the Norwegian crown, the Sagas subsequently drifted down into only semi-reliable records; and later were little less historical than the half-fiction, half-fact of the Saga-writer of modern times—Sir Walter Scott.

The modern historical romances of this author belong

to the same class of literature as the Sagas; but with
this difference: in the former, the historical element is
subservient to fiction, while in the Sagas it plays the
principal part. The Sagas that may be considered,
for the most part, historical are those written down
up to the end of the fourteenth century.

It is for its originality that the Icelandic Saga
Literature stands out pre-eminent among the litera-
tures of Europe, and even of the world. For the
most part the Icelanders did not draw from other
wells than those they found belonging to their own
countrymen—their own Northern race—whether the
actual events happened at home, as in Niála; or
abroad, as in Olaf Tryggvason's Saga, the Saga of
Harald Haardrada, and many many more. The Icelanders, however, were among the most active people
of early mediæval Europe. Their solitary situation
and long winter—and their winters they generally
spent at home, devoting simply the summer months to
their Viking expeditions—gave a peculiar facility for
recording, in their eight months' winter, their four
mouths' summer experience cruising about the high
seas, making raids in their dragon-prowed ships far
and wide, being hospitably treated at friendly Courts,
and fighting hard battles with their enemies. These
Northern sea-rovers were just in the position to be
splendid historians, and so they proved. Their life
was one ring of excitement, they drank with their
friends and fought with their foes, they roamed from
land to land and brought back stores of information
and scenes of the most stirring adventure to relate to
their stay-at-home kinsmen in the far Northern Isle;
and these wanderers on the wide ocean were most
warmly welcomed when in the autumn-time they re-
turned. There was frequently a jealousy among the
kinsmen, when a sea-rover came back to his native
sysla or district, as to who should have the honour
of housing him during the winter, and all vied with
one another in showing him the utmost hospitality.

That is still, to a certain extent, the case at present in Iceland. Living solitary lives, the peasants and families take a particular delight in welcoming a stranger within their walls, and hasten to serve him with coffee—and delicious coffee it is too—so that then they may sit themselves down and hear the news. And when Icelanders meet on the road—there are no roads in Iceland, by-the-bye, so we should say on the bridle-paths, for all travelling in Iceland is accomplished on sturdy, sure-footed little ponies—they pull up and make a long halt, not unfrequently for a good hour or two, before proceeding on their respective routes.

Time now, no more than it was in the olden days, is an affair not at all taken notice of; and it is still a custom up country, where books are scarce, for the borrower of a book or MS., before sending it back, to copy the contents out, word for word. In this way the whole of the winter evenings are sometimes spent; in fact an amusement of the kind is almost necessary, as they are frequently snowed up, and so bound to stay in doors. So it was in the days gone by, and these long winters assisted considerably in the creation of the Icelandic literature; and that this rich and rare literature has been preserved to posterity is in a measure due to the solitary sea-girt situation of the land, and the next-door-to-no-communication that still is a great feature in Iceland. The Icelanders have not even yet constructed roads in their land, and until they do this the country is likely to present the same appearance a thousand years hence as it did in the days of Bergthora and Niál.

Iceland has always been a land apart. Italy, France, Germany, England, Holland, Belgium, and other "geographical expressions," have borrowed one from another, rubbed shoulders together, and each succeeding century since the days of the early Italian Renaissance—the days of Dante and Boccaccio—has so changed as scarcely to be able to recognise the one that immediately went before. It is totally different in Iceland. There the fashions are much about the same as they were in the time of the Sagas, for, in a land devoid of roads, what chance is there of dragging over the mountains and through the wild desert lava-wastes, ponies being the only means of conveyance, more than the actual necessities of daily life? The country is even less fertile now than it was then, for we read in the Sagas that, in the neighbourhood of Hekla, where now there is nothing but sand and lava-stones, formerly there flourished verdant plains, with sheep browsing in every direction.

The Icelanders have not yet been favoured with a Cæsar to teach them that the making of roads is the first step to progress in what the Roman Conqueror then called, and we still call—MODERN CIVILISATION.

It is no wonder, then, that with these difficulties of communication staring the Icelanders in the face, that the language, only a spoken language up to the middle of the 12th century, and then written down with exceeding purity, and amazing grammatical skill in the 12th, 13th, and 14th, should have remained almost unchanged even up to the present day.

And of this fact the Icelanders are particularly proud. Niála, or Niálssaga, is generally considered the most important of these old Icelandic records; it shows clearly and distinctly the warlike and passionate spirit that ruled during the most stirring times in Iceland, and the scene of the Saga is in the neighbourhood round about Thingvellir, the ancient seat of the Icelandic Parliament, and in the whole country the most classic ground. Here, on the plains of Thingvellir, the Assembly met annually, uninterruptedly for nearly a thousand years—925-1800 A.D. Many of the most distinguished families in Iceland who lived between 970 and 1017, the period of Niálssaga, play a part therein, and for a description of Icelandic social and political life it is second to none. It was among the first of the Sagas written down, probably in the latter half of the 12th century, or the commencement of the 13th.

To show that the spirit of poetry has not quite fled from the birth-land of so 'many skálds and Saga-writers, this is the Hymn of Welcome that greeted His Majesty the King of Denmark, on arriving at Thingvellir, to take part in the Icelandic Millenary Festival of 1874, and to increase on this occasion the joy of his Icelandic subjects by granting them a free constitution. This event was very appropriately mentioned by the Vice-President of the Royal Society of Northern Antiquaries at Copenhagen as affording material for a new King's Saga.* I was there, and as the Hymn re-echoed among the mountains, the effect was grand in the extreme.

The original is by Matthias Jochumsson. Some of you might have a little difficulty in understanding the Icelandic, so I will ask you to be satisfied with my English translation :—

Plant thy firm foot on Iceland's holy plain ;
  We welcome thee, most noble-hearted King,
First of all Denmark's monarchs dost thou deign
  To visit our wild mountains, and to bring
The light of Liberty to our dear land :
  We welcome thee, O King, with heart and hand.

O Iceland's father, go to yonder hill,
  The Lögberg, and thence gaze on all around :
The fire-wrought ramparts, waters blue and still
  In the deep chasms, listen to the sound
Of leaping torrents, in the nation's ear
  They whisper "Freedom hath her Altar here."

Ye hoary clefts of Iceland's hallowed shrine !
  Ye mountains, and ye valleys, as of yore
Re-echo thro' the land the voice divine
  Of Freedom, and 'twill sound from shore to shore.
For, to our nation still this spirit clings,
  And welcomes thee, belovèd, best of kings.

---

* *Vide* speech of the Vice-President of the Royal Society of Northern Antiquaries, J. J. A. Worsaae, at the 50th Anniversary Festival, held on January 28th, 1875, in the Palace of the Amalienborg, presided over by the King of Denmark, Christian IX., President of the Society.

And, tho' a thousand years are passed since we
  First found a dwelling in this Northern clime,
Our nation, ever struggling to be free,
  Hath battled bravely 'gainst the roll of Time;
And in thy coming, King, we hail the dawn
  For Iceland, of a brighter happier morn.

May yet, O King, thy name a thousand years.
  Live with the good conferred on us to-day!
So long as Hekla his proud summit rears,
  And Geysir growls and scatters boiling spray,
May the Almighty Father shower down
  His blessings on *thee* and on Denmark's crown.

A few words now with regard to the MSS. themselves. In the Royal Library of Copenhagen there is preserved the most ancient copy of the Elder or Poetical Edda. Bishop Sveinsson—Brynjúlf Sveinsson, of Skálholt—discovered at his Episcopal seat in the year 1643 an old parchment, that, on closer examination, proved to be a Codex, containing the most important of the Edda songs.

This Codex Regius as it is called, from the character of the handwriting or *script,* and other distinguishing marks, may be set down as a MS. of the latter part of the 13th century. It is called Codex Regius because it was sent by Bishop Sveinsson, of Skálholt, to King Frederick III. of Denmark, who in reality was the founder of the Royal Library at Copenhagen. This patron of learning purchased three large private libraries, those of Gersdorf, Ulfeld, and Scavenius, and sent the most renowned literary men about his Court to travel in foreign lands, to search after rare books and MSS., and particularly to make themselves acquainted with the libraries at that time the most celebrated in Europe.

It was Frederick III. of Denmark who intimated to Bishop Sveinsson, Torfæus, and other scholarly Icelanders about the Court, his wish to procure for the Royal Library some Icelandic books and MSS., and this is how the Royal Library came to possess the earliest copies extant of the two Eddas, many interesting and important Saga MSS., law codes, and historical records from Iceland.

In the Royal Library may also be seen one of the most richly-illuminated Icelandic MSS.—the Flatey-arbók — commonly called in Copenhagen the Codex Flateyensis. Brynjúlf Sveinsson, with great difficulty, and not a little diplomacy, procured this rare and interesting book — one of the jewels of the Library—from a farmer, Jonas Torfason, dwelling at Flatey, or Flat Island, in the Breiðafjord, on the western coast of Iceland.

The farmer was extremely loth to part with this magnificent vellum, that had been handed down in the family for many generations, and was looked upon as a kind of heirloom or household god. The Bishop, however, used his powers of persuasion, and the farmer was induced to hand it over to the King, on condition that he should pay no more King's taxes for the rest of his life. Frederick III. granted to the farmer this privilege, and thus both made a good bargain, especially the farmer, who held one of the largest farms at that time in Iceland.

It is not of a particularly early date—circa. 1395 A.D.—but in these two large folio volumes are contained many of the most important Sagas, to wit, Olaf Tryggvason's Saga, the Saga of Olaf the Saint, Orkneyinga Saga, Hákon Hákonsson's Saga, the Saga of Magnus the Good, and of Harald Haardrada, Grænlendinga Tháttr, Edward the Confessor's Saga, and lastly, a historical account from the creation of the world to the year of grace A.D. 1395 ! ! !

How far this last is correct in every detail it would be perhaps rather dangerous to say; we can say, however, that quaint and beautiful are the illuminations and valuable is the work, because containing so many interesting and important records.

The text, however, is not to be too much relied upon, as the scribes of the Flateyarbók, two monks in collating from the earlier MSS. have been most inaccurate, and used frequent abbreviations to save time as well as trouble, and so have made their book extremely difficult to read, even by good Icelandic scholars. The earlier the MS., generally speaking, the simpler and the more legible is the hand, each word being written clearly, distinctly, and in full.

Also in the Royal Library is shown the earliest specimen known of any written record in the old Northern or Icelandic tongue. It is merely a leaf, a list of priests' names, and the date of this leaf, that was found bound up in a book of a later period, is set down as about 1150 A.D., for at the foot there is a statement that says it was written immediately after the death of the last-named priest, whom we know, from other records, died in 1143. Rarely was it the custom in Iceland for the Saga writers to put either name or date to their MSS.; they simply recorded what they had to tell, and as the books were frequently written by several members of a family, or copies of earlier MSS., this omission is easily accounted for. However, the respective dates of Icelandic MSS. may be rather accurately ascertained; first, by the character of the handwriting, for instance, the various formations of the letter d, and secondly, by the manner and mode of abbreviation.

Beyond this one leaf, all the MSS. that have escaped destruction are of considerably later date, viz., from the 13th and 14th centuries. There are a few from the latter part of the 12th century, but they are, for the most part, homilies or lives of saints, and so forth; works that have but little or no importance when considering Icelandic literature. There is, however, among these one Icelandic MS. that may be of interest to Englishmen—it contains the life of Thomas à Becket, Archbishop of Canterbury, but is, no doubt, merely a translation into Icelandic from the Latin record preserved in the Episcopal Library at Lambeth.

But although there are the earliest known speci-
mens of Icelandic MSS. to be met with in the Royal
Library, yet in the University Library of Copenhagen
is the grand collection made by Arni Magnússon at
the commencement of the 18th century.

Arnas Magnæus as he is sometimes called—it was the
fashion in the 17th and 18th centuries for literary men
to Latinise their names—occupied ten years of his life
(1702-12) travelling in Iceland from farm to farm,
collecting any MSS. the peasant farmers might have
in their possession; he travelled as an "Embedsmand"
or Danish official, and so the facilities were great for
acquiring these valuable records, at that time stored
away in dark corners of the farmers' huge oaken chests,
or lying about covered over perhaps with a century of
dust on the little book-shelves over the door of the
guest chamber in the farm-houses or "bærs." Many
of the MSS. were unfortunately burnt in the great
fire that occurred in Copenhagen in the year 1728.
It is difficult to say what was destroyed in this disas-
trous conflagration—possibly a far older transcript of
the Edda Songs than the Codex Regius in the Royal
Library. Two years after this Arni Magnússon, who
for some years had held the appointment of Principal
Librarian in the University Library of Copenhagen,
died, and by his last will and testament bequeathed
this unique collection of nearly 1,600 Icelandic MSS.
to his Alma Mater. The most important of these
MSS. is a well-penned and perfect Codex of the
Younger or Snorri Edda.

Belonging to the first part of the 14th century is
the Codex of Snorri Sturluson's grand work entitled
Heimskríngla, "home round," or rather "round
home," *heimur* literally meaning world—lat. *mundus,*
—and *kríngla,* a disc or plate.

Philosophers at that period of the world's history
believed the earth to be a round flat like a plate, and
this celebrated saga-work of Snorri's is a true and
faithful account of the life and times of the old Nor-

wegian kings. For no inconsiderable portion of that work, however, Snorri Sturluson was, as he himself acknowledges in the preface, indebted to Ari Fróði, the author of the Islendingabók (*Schedæ libellus de Islandiá*), and of the Landnámabók, or book of the colonisation. This last-mentioned work corresponds in some measure to our Doomsday Book.

With regard to the caligraphy of this Codex of the Heimskríngla, much better it is not possible to find, although as a rule the more ancient the MS. the more clear and beautiful is the handwriting, the formation of the letters, and the penmanship. In later times these good qualities diminish, and the "script" becomes more like the Gothic or Old German.

Simple and artistic and well-coloured are the illuminations to the Heimskríngla, they are bold and broad in treatment.

Other MSS. there are, penned perhaps in as masterly a style, but from this copy of the Heimskríngla a very fair idea can be formed of the manner of recording the historical facts and traditions prevalent among the Icelanders in former times.

There is an interesting study in the future, and one that has already been commenced by an Icelandic scholar in Copenhagen, viz., the drawing of comparisons between some of the plays of Shakespeare and the old Northern writings, for of the whole row of European authors from the renaissance of literature down to the present time Shakespeare is the only one who reproduces that fine touch of tragic spirit as found in Gudrun's kvíða, Atlamál, and others of the Edda Songs.

This pure Northern spirit in the dramas of Shakespeare is chiefly to be traced in Macbeth, by some critics considered the *chef d'œuvre* of all Shakespeare's plays, is apparent in no small degree in Richard III. and King Lear, and occurs occasionally in Hamlet. But this, however, is a subject for itself and a wide one too.

In Gunnlaug's Saga Ormstúnga we get enlightened as to how far the Old Northern language of the 10th and 11th centuries was the language of the British Isles.

Before William of Normandy came to our shores, and brought about a change in the language of England by the introduction of the *valska*, the Saga says there was one tongue in England as in Denmark and Norway—*Ein var þá túnga á Englandi sem í Danmörku ok Noregi.*   This referred to the time when Ethelred was king over England, and it was in the winter of the year 1006 that Gunnlaug, having composed a poem in the king's honour, came to the Anglo-Saxon Court, and craved permission, in the Royal presence, to recite his poem. Permission was granted, and the king was so well satisfied that he gave this Northern *skáld* a place in his own body-guard, a great honour, and one highly appreciated in those days. The poets were the historians of that age, and kings and chieftains, loving to hear their praises sung, and careful that their brave battle-deeds should be handed down to posterity, gave gifts of great price to their poets and a foremost seat among the retainers at their Court.

In Olaf Tryggvason's Saga will be found some interesting particulars regarding the attack on London in the days of the Old Norse Vikings. How Olaf and Sweyn came to Londonbury, on the nativity of St. Mary the Virgin, with 590 ships, and set fire to the city—how the stout burghers faced their predatory foes and kept them back. Nevertheless, they wrought the most evil that ever any host did here by burning, harrying, and manslaughter. Then the king (Ethelred) paid them £16,000 to go away, and Olaf promised that he never to England more would come with unpeace.*   Unpeace was the expression in the old Northern language for war.   It

---

* Unpeace—Icel. *ófrið.*

was after this raid upon London that Olaf built the church in Southwark that is called St. Olave's to this day. Tooley Street is nothing more than St. Ole Street—Ole being the Norse abbreviation for the more dignified Olaf.

The visit of the Northmen to the Court of King Athelstan is spoken of in Egilssaga. Egill Skalla-grímsson, one of the most renowned of Icelandic *skálds*, fought side by side with Athelstan at the battle of Brunaburgh against the Scots.

And we also read in the Sagas about the foundation of the cathedral church of St. Paul's, about the year 610, by Ethelred, King of Kent, who gave the land to St. Paul's Monastery, and how the edifice was entirely destroyed by a fearful fire that devastated London in 1086. Many of our early English customs are constantly referred to—for instance, the salving of the kings. Harald II. was, on the 8th day of July, 1066, salved—*i.e.*, smeared over with a sweet smelling ointment—in St. Paul's Church—(var vígðr konungsvígslu í Páls kírkju.)*

In Knytlinga Saga, in Egilssaga, Orkneyinga Saga there are pages and pages of matter of the highest historical importance to England.

The best side of the English character comes from the connection with the Vikings, the sea-rovers of the 9th, 10th, and 11th centuries, and their descendants. They taught our countrymen pluck, bravery, and independence. They ravaged our coasts, intermarried with our people, and their children's children have been those who tended most, when our nation was in its prime, to make the name of England ring round from shore to shore. Drake, Frobisher, and Shakespeare are names of Scandinavian origin, and it will be remembered our great dramatic poet gave to his son the beautiful Northern name of Hamet.

IRELAND.—It is a well-known fact that the Scandi-

---

* Harald Haardrada's Saga, c. 112. Fornmanna Sögur, vi. 396.

navian sea-rovers often found their way to Ireland, and fought not unfrequently with the Irish kings—sometimes for them, sometimes against them, according to circumstances or fate—fate, in this instance, meaning principally pay or promises of reward.

It will also be remembered that King Olaf Tryggvason, who plays so conspicuous a *rôle* in the history of the Norwegian kings, married an Irish princess, and before being recalled to his native Norway, to assume there the reins of government, was for sometime King of Dublin. This was in the latter part of the 10th century.

AMERICA.—In the Flateyarbók, the Codex Flateyensis previously referred to, may be found the history of Eric the Red (Eiríkr Rauði), the discoverer of Greenland, and also much that is interesting and important regarding the discovery of America by the Icelandic sea-rovers in the 10th century.* Eric the Red founded a colony in Greenland, and it was his son Leif—commonly called Leif the Lucky—(Leifr Heppni) returning to Greenland from an expedition to Norway, was drifted out of his course by adverse winds and carried away from the Greenland coast down on to the American shore as far south as the present Massachusetts. In the days of the Vikings this land was known as Vínland†.—Vineland—because Leif and his party found, on landing, grapes growing there in abundance.

It is wonderful where these Icelandic and Norse sea-rovers penetrated in the 10th century with their dragon-prowed barks. As above seen, Greenland they first discovered and colonised; then America, five hundred years before the Genoese navigator sailed out into the West; and even there is a tradition among the Indians in the backwoods of Honduras

---

* Eric the Red's statue in bronze has been erected in New York, thus giving tangible proof of the respect the Americans have for the early sea-roving Vikings who visited their shores.

† Adam of Bremen's MSS.. 11th century, Biblio. Imp., Vienna, and Antiquitatis Americanæ, C. C. Rafn, 1837.

and Yucatan that three or four centuries before the
Spanish sailors landed on American soil, was known
a race of people with blue eyes and fair hair.   Can it
not be that the people to whom this tradition refers
were Northmen from Iceland, for why should these
sea-rovers content themselves' with coasting along
the shores of Markland, Vineland, and Sloeland?
It is a natural inference that as in the year 1000 A.D.
these daring and adventurous sea-faring folk set foot
in America and settled there, they or their after-
comers, without any vast improbability, could have
sailed farther south, and, crossing the Gulf of Mexico,
made friends with the Indians in the dark forests of
Honduras and Yucatan.   This is an interesting and
entirely new point; it is one that deserves more than
a passing thought, more especially as it does not
emanate from the high seats of Scandinavian learning,
but is a tradition still current in the backwoods of
Central America among the Indians themselves.

It is a well-known fact that Columbus was more
than once in Bristol port.   Now in his day whalers
there were not a few in Bristol who had been up in
the Northern seas, and had come back with many of
the old Norse traditions in their heads and on their
tongues.   While on their Northern voyages they
often touched at Reykjavik, the capital of Iceland,
in the south-west part of the Island, for in its bay
refuge may be taken from the terrific storms
that so frequently occur in the North Atlantic,
and probably there heard the Icelanders tell of a
vast continent out in the West which had been discovered and colonised by their renowned' ancestors,
the wild sea-faring Vikings.   This was just such
a story as the Bristol whalers were likely to re-
member, and there is nothing more probable than
but they told it over and over again in the taverns
on their return home and by "their ain firesides."

Columbus in this way might easily have been a
listener, and turned over in his own mind whether

a voyage should not be undertaken to Iceland in order to hear more closely about these traditions, and to gather as much information as possible about this talked-of land in the West. To a man of thought there is always something peculiarly interesting in traditionary lore. It opens up a wide field for speculative reasoning. Columbus is supposed to have landed in Iceland in the month of February, 1477, and even the spot where he first set foot on Icelandic soil was pointed out to me during my recent stay in Iceland by some fisherfolk who dwell on a ness in the neighbourhood of Reykjavik.

The Icelanders are a tradition-loving people, and in the 15th century their traditions had not been weakened by the introduction of the printing press.

It is only in comparatively later times that the Sagas containing the written accounts of this early colonisation of America have been brought to light; but even in the time of Columbus they must have existed, though known to nobody out of Iceland, probably not even to the possessors themselves.

There is far more important matter in these Icelandic Sagas than people generally believe, and it is not altogether improbable that the farmer who possessed either Eyrbyggja Saga or Thorfinn's Saga* might have communicated their contents to Columbus, and so have given rise to the boldness of his proposals, first to the Court of Genoa and then to that of Spain.

And in conclusion I would say that, for the better understanding of the literature of Iceland, there is nothing like taking a tour in the country itself; it is the only country in the world with a grand classical literature that has not been materially affected by the inroads of modern civilisation, by the different waves of literature and art that have been in succeeding centuries the remodeller, as it were, of neighbouring

---

* These two Sagas contain the History of the Discovery by the Icelanders of Greenland in the year 982 and of America 1000 A.D.

lands, as well as the native ground where it had sprung up; but Iceland has remained outwardly the same; the language, for eight or ten centuries, has undergone little alteration, only the active pictures of the inward social and political life have faded away, and the devastating effects of the frequent volcanic eruptions have made barren and unfruitful many spots that were well cultivated in the days when the Icelandic chieftains rode in such splendour and pride to the meetings of the Althing on the plains of Thingvellir, and her scalds and heroes were the talk of the age, and welcome at every European Court.

Nations are like individuals, they grow up from small beginnings, enter upon their youth, burst forth in the full blossoming of manhood and strength, grow old, and pass away; and again, like individuals, if their work be good work, they leave a treasure to posterity in their footprints on the sands of time.